Good Night, Sleep Tight, Little Bunnies

For my friend Louis, with love
—D.A.

ISBN 0-439-53070-9

12 11 10 9 8 7 6 5 4 3 2 1   3 4 5 6 7 8/0

Printed in the U.S.A.   23

First Scholastic paperback printing, February 2003

Good Night, Sleep Tight, Little Bunnies

Dawn Apperley

Cartwheel ·B·O·O·K·S· ®

SCHOLASTIC INC.

New York   Toronto   London   Auckland   Sydney
Mexico City   New Delhi   Hong Kong   Buenos Aires

Stars are out,
The moon shines bright,
The time has come
To say good night.

Hidden in the meadow,
Among the pretty flowers,
Little bunnies dream away
The long night hours.
Good night, sleep tight,
little bunnies.

Deep in the forest,
In the starry night,
Little monkey is asleep—
Mama holds her tight.
Good night, sleep tight,
little monkey.

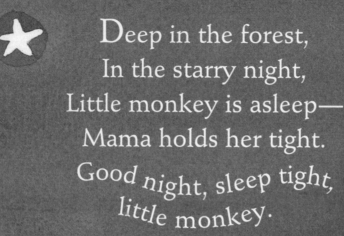

High on a branch,
In a small twig nest,
Little birds are ready
For a good night's rest.
Good night, sleep tight,
little birds.

Away in the desert,
With her eyes shut tight,
Little camel sleeps—
Here's a kiss good night.
Good night, sleep tight,
little camel.

In the tall brown grass,
With her long gray nose,
Little elephant is snoring
While she takes a doze.
Good night, sleep tight,
little elephant.

Over by the pond,
Tucked away among the reeds,
Little ducks are fast asleep,
Sheltered from the breeze.
Good night, sleep tight,
little ducks.

In the land of snow,
Cuddled up on daddy's feet,
Little penguin's happy,
Fast, fast asleep.

Good night, sleep tight,
little penguin.

Deep in the jungle,
All cozy in a huddle,
Little tigers lie so still,
Purring as they cuddle.
Good night, sleep tight,
little tigers.

At the bottom of the ocean,
When it's very late,
Little octopus is wrapped in arms—
Not one, not two, but eight!
Good night, sleep tight,
little octopus.

Home in their cave,
All warm and snug,
Little bears are sharing
A big bear hug.
Good night, sleep tight,
little bears.

I tuck you in your bed
And turn out the light,
I wish you sweet dreams
And hug you good night.
Good night, little one,
sleep tight.